THE DAY
I BECAME
THE MOST
WANTED
BOY IN THE WORLD

THE DAY I BECAME THE MOST WANTED BOY IN THE WORLD

TOM MCLAUGHLIN

WALKER
BOOKS

First published in Great Britain 2018 by Walker Books Ltd
87 Vauxhall Walk, London SE11 5HJ

2 4 6 8 10 9 7 5 3 1

Text and illustrations © 2018 Tom McLaughlin
Cover design © 2018 Walker Books Ltd

This book has been typeset in Stempel Schneidler

Printed and bound in Great Britain by CPI Group (UK) Ltd

British Library Cataloguing in Publication Data:
a catalogue record for this book is available from the British Library

ISBN 978-1-4063-7580-0

www.walker.co.uk

To my beautiful wife, who really likes getting a dedication in as many books as she possibly can.

1 p.m.

"This man is dangerous. Probably the most dangerous in the entire world. What's he going to do? He's taking his time and...

What a safety shot for Mark Shelby! He really does have John Wiggins on the ropes."

"These two heavyweights have been duking it out for the last half hour and not one ball has been potted. I hope you're enjoying this as much at home as we are in the commentary box."

"YES!" Pete gasped. "I'm so excited I can hardly breathe!"

For Pete, snooker was a passion. It was right up there with rearranging his sock drawer and having a nice sit-down. While others bungee-jumped off bridges or free-climbed cliffs with little more than a pair of trainers and a silly haircut, Pete's adrenaline ride was a thrill-a-minute roller coaster of snooker balls, chalk and softly spoken commentators.

Nothing, but nothing was going to interrupt his afternoon in front of his tiny TV.

"PEEEETE?"

yelled his mum. "Pete! Can you hear me?!"

"Why can't they give me a moment's peace?" Pete huffed as he got up from the bean bag that he'd carefully plumped, squeezed and moulded, ready for an afternoon of white-knuckle excitement.

"Yes, Mother?" Pete replied. He always called his mum "Mother" when he was annoyed with her.

"Less of the 'Mother' malarkey. I need parsnips," she called up the stairs of their small home in Barnet. Pete and his mum and dad had always lived here; it was on the edge of the city and the edge of any excitement.

Pete's dad, Malcolm used to be in the Navy before becoming a washing-machine salesman in a local store. This was where he met Pete's mum, Diane. She was a fridge saleswoman at the time, and soon their love blossomed in the electrical appliances department.

"I'm making parsnip and cheese bake," Mum continued as Pete plodded down the stairs, "and without parsnips, it's just a bowl of hot cheese. I need you to go to the shops." She handed Pete a bag-for-life, a handful of coins and a shopping list.

"Can't Dad do it?" Pete asked, his voice whining with frustration. "There's a terrific match on TV – any minute now someone might even pot a ball."

"No. Whenever your father goes to the shops, he goes rogue. Remember the time I sent him out for stamps and he came back with an exercise bike? Besides which, he's in the middle of tending to his hanging tulip." Mum rolled her eyes and pointed out of the window.

There was Dad in the front garden, watering can in one hand, feather duster in the other. "Would you like some water, Gertrude?" Dad smiled, giving the flower a little dust.

"He's naming them now." Mum sighed. "I caught him talking about a Jemima in his sleep the other day. I was about to wallop him when I realized he was talking about one of his roses." Mum paused and looked Pete up and down. "What are you wearing and where did you find those clothes?"

"Oh, erm, nothing. It was the first thing I found in the wardrobe," he said sheepishly.

Pete was dressed in a large shirt, bow tie and waistcoat – just like a snooker player.

The outfits were one of the many reasons he liked the game; the players dressed in a way that added to the sense of occasion.

Pete wondered what it would be like if other sports took their appearance as seriously as snooker players. Surely the world would be a better place if footballers wore tweed and racing drivers sported cravats and sensible shoes.

"Which wardrobe?" Mum asked and folded her arms. "Have you been going through your dad's stuff again? You know he doesn't like it when you dress in his clothes. Have you forgotten that time you borrowed his white shirt and he saw you coming down the stairs in the dark and thought it was his own ghost?!" Mum shook her head. "I had to chase him around the house for half an hour before I could convince him otherwise."

"Well, if you'd just buy me my own snooker outfit I wouldn't have to!" Pete snapped.

"There's no such thing!" Mum said. "I go into shops and ask for it and they look at me like I've gone loopy.

Oh, Pete … maybe if you wore normal clothes you might make a friend or two? Wouldn't that be wonderful?"

"Bye Mum!" Pete said, folding the shopping list and tucking it into the shallow pocket of his waistcoat; a place normally reserved for a square of snooker chalk.

It was true that Pete didn't have any friends. He once had a childhood friend, but that ended when he pushed Pete down a bumpy slide in the local park – resulting in not one, but two grazed knees. Ever since then, Pete, like the Arctic wolf, preferred to operate alone.

"Remember the parsnips and the other bits and bobs that I've written down on the list!" Mum shouted after him.

"Fine!" Pete snorted and headed for the front door. "I bet Mark Shelby never had to put up with this."

He stashed the change in his trouser pocket, scrunched the bag-for-life under his arm and narrowed his eyes as the bright of day hit him square in the face.

"DON'T MOVE, OR I'LL BLAST YOU INTO NEXT WEEK!"

said a voice from behind a bush in the garden.

2 p.m.

"Take my money, my trousers – take it all! JUST DON'T HURT ME!" Pete wailed.

There was a moment of silence, then Pete got a soaking of epic proportions and promptly fell to the ground.

"HAHA!" the voice yelled and started to laugh.

Pete shook his head the way a dog would after getting out of the bath. He wiped the water from his face, eyed up the dastardly villain and slowly got up. There, on the grass in front of him was a small boy. He was holding a huge water pistol that was almost twice his size, covered in silver plastic telescopes and levers – it could almost have been the real thing. The boy had stopped laughing and now had a very worried look on his face. He was called Sammy, otherwise known to Pete as his massively annoying next-door neighbour.

"I'M COMPLETELY SOAKED, YOU LITTLE NINCOMPOOP!"

Pete yelled. "I've got a good mind to tell your parents, you … you scoundrel!" Even Pete was shocked by how cross he was.

Sammy backed away to the pavement. Pete stumbled towards him, rubbing his eyes, which were still stinging from the water.

"LOOK OUT!"

Sammy shouted. Pete suddenly felt himself being knocked over. He barely had time to yell "argh" before he fell again.

"Oi!" a man blurted out as he collided with Pete, sending his bag-for-life and shopping list flying through the air. The man quickly got up and brushed himself down. "You need to watch where you're going, kid," he sneered. He looked like a man not to be messed with. Dark stubble covered half his face, and he was wearing a pork-pie hat, a bow tie and a coat pulled up around his neck, like he was expecting rain.

"I'm so sorry. I had water in my eyes," Pete explained.

"SORRY!" Sammy shouted and ran over. "It was my fault. I was playing with my friend, Pete."

"Wait ... we're not friends—" Pete started, pausing to pick up his bag-for-life and shopping list from the pavement.

"I don't care how youse know each other," the man said in a gravelly voice. "Just get out of my way, understand?" He pushed the boys aside and started to carefully scan the pavement.

Pete turned around and noticed a piece of paper on the front lawn. "Oh, were you looking for this?" he asked and picked it up.

"Fanks," the man said. He stomped over and grabbed the paper before making a hasty retreat.

"Well he seemed a bit grumpy, hey, friend?" Sammy said and shrugged. "Hi, Pete, how are you? I wondered if you wanted to come round and play KerPlunk with me some time? I tried to ask you at school, but you sort of blanked me and then ran away," Sammy gabbled on.

"STOP CALLING ME FRIEND!"

Pete snapped. "You're not my friend. Friends don't shoot water in each other's face. I could have grazed a knee ... or worse!"

"What?" Sammy laughed. "Sorry about shooting you in the face. I was just trying out my new water pistol. Do you want to squirt some old tin cans off the wall with me? Or we could play something else?" Sammy continued, trying to ignore Pete's unenthusiastic expression. "I have a PlayStation, or we could kick around a football, or we could ... you know ... dress up and play waiters," Sammy said, looking at Pete's outfit.

Pete was horrified. "I'm not pretending to be a waiter – I'm dressed as a snooker player. When kids wear football kits no one laughs at them – why should snooker be any different?"

"Classic pal banter." Sammy chuckled. "So, let's play snooker then. They have a

table in the youth club down the road –
we could go there?"

"That is a POOL TABLE! How dare you
confuse the two games!" Pete shouted.

"Oh, OK, sorry... They are *sort* of the
same game," Sammy muttered under his
breath.

"SAMMY, FOR THE LAST TIME: WE'RE NOT FRIENDS!"

Pete said suddenly. "I'm sorry, but you're
in the year below me, and even if you
weren't, I'm not looking for any more
friends at the moment. This just won't
work out; it's you ... not me."

"What? Why?" Sammy shouted as he
chased after Pete.

"Hanging out with someone younger isn't *cool* and I don't want to look *uncool*."

"Says the boy dressed like an eighteenth-century duke."

"Dapper... I look dapper."

"What does *dapper* mean?" Sammy asked and scratched his head.

"It means smart. It means ... this!" Pete said, gesturing at his outfit. "Now, if you'll excuse me, I'm off to buy some parsnips and other bits and bobs." Pete turned and bounded off towards the corner shop.

"Great! I was going to the shops anyway." Sammy smiled.

"Liar!" Pete called out.

"YOU'RE FOLLOWING ME. STOP FOLLOWING ME!"

"I'm not. It's a free country – I'll do what I want, mate."

"I am not your mate, or your friend, pal or anything like that," Pete grumbled.

"WILL YOU STOP FOLLOWING ME! JUST STOP IT!!!"

The gruff man with the stubbly face looked at the two boys arguing in the distance and shook his head.

"Stupid kids," he muttered before turning the corner and heading towards an old van that was parked there. He checked no one was around then, with a yank, he slid the creaky door open and climbed into the back. It was full of other gruff-looking men who all had stubbly faces and were all wearing hats and bow ties. This was no ordinary van; this was the getaway vehicle for the Blodder Brothers, London's most notorious criminal gang. There wasn't a crime in the city that couldn't somehow be traced back to the family.

From robberies to jewellery heists or stealing cars, there wasn't an unsavoury pie that the Blodder Gang didn't have their particularly grubby fingers stuck in.

The not-to-be-messed-with-looking man that Pete and Sammy had run into happened to be Baz Blodder, the eldest of the brothers and a professional robber who had just been released from prison

for holding up a post office. And now, he was ready to get the Blodder Gang back in business in Barnet. In the front of the van sat Bob, the driver and Blake, who shifted the gear. In the back of the van was Bill, who liked to hit people; Brad, the weapons man and finally Brody, the safe-cracker. There was a Bertie too, but he'd turned his back on a life of crime to take up ballroom dancing in Blackpool, and was currently ranked number three in the whole of the UK.

"Sorry I'm late," Baz said. "I had a run in wiv two runts. Anyways, I've walked the streets and there's no sign of Old Bill."

"I'm 'ere," Bill said waving.

"Nah, Old Bill is a synonym for the police," Baz corrected his younger brother.

"Oh yeah, course. That makes more sense," Bill replied.

"So we're all good. We all know the drill. We go in. Bob waits by the wheel. I 'and over the note asking for the cash so no one will 'ear our voices. Then they give us the money and we leave. It should be the perfect crime. Blake, give out the masks," Baz ordered.

Blake reached into a bag and handed one out to everyone.

"What are these?" Bob asked. "I fought we said clown masks – clown masks are scary, they instill a sense of ... foreboding."

"They were out of clown masks," Blake said. "It was this or nuffin."

"Isn't that...?" Bill asked, as he looked at the mask.

"Yep, the expert vegetable grower and second-in-line to the throne, Prince Charles," Blake confirmed.

"A mask's a mask. It don't matter what we look like. Worst comes to worst, maybe they'll pin the bank job on 'im," Brad added.

"You make a good point," Baz agreed. "Now, let's get to work," he snarled.

The Blodder Gang lowered their masks over their faces and the van sped towards the bank.

3 p.m.

Pete looked over his shoulder to
find Sammy trailing along behind him
like an eager puppy. "You're still here,"
he sighed.

"I told you, I'm just walking this way
too. It's a complete coincidence."

Pete suddenly stopped. As did Sammy.
Pete ran on ahead as fast as he could. As
did Sammy. Pete started zigzagging across
the pavement. As did Sammy.

"What is wrong with you? Stop following me! Stop copying me!"

"I'm not following you. I always walk this way to the shop – it's just a massive, spooky coincidence that you do too!" Sammy cried. "Out of interest, how many friends *do* you have?"

"I have five friends actually," Pete snapped back.

"Wow, OK, you know the exact number – that's … organized. Well, now you have six. If you keep this up you may well get to ten by the time you're forty!"

"I don't need six!" Pete protested. "I have Steve – the boy I sit next to in Maths – he is very funny … well, not funny, but he's kind and he lets me borrow his calculator … or at least he did once. What a guy! Then there's Nan. Number three is—"

"Whoa-whoa-whoa! Did you say … 'Nan'?" Sammy asked, stopping in his tracks.

"No," Pete said, realizing that he had made a huge mistake.

"You did! Who are the others – your mum and dad and your teddy?"

Pete was silent.

"Oh … my … word, they are! You can't count your relatives as your friends! It's a good job I found you. I can help you," Sammy said reassuringly.

"I can have who I want as friends. I get to choose – that's the point of friends, isn't it? And, for your information, my nan is a hoot and a brilliant Boggle player, who makes excellent cakes and sings like an angel."

"You *sing* to each other?" Sammy was horrified.

"Will you stop looking at me like that?" Pete protested. "We do sometimes... It passes the time before Countdown starts."

"It's OK. As your friend I understand, and I am not here to judge … but maybe we shouldn't be friends after all. I have a lot of street cred in this town – I don't want it to vanish overnight."

"I'm cool!" Pete said, losing his temper. "I do cool things! I once did a wheelie on my bike that lasted nearly a second, and a girl was watching and she winked at me."

"Was it your nan?"

"NO IT WASN'T!"

"OK, that does sound cool. I've thought it over and I'm prepared to put this behind us. I do however have a few ground rules that are best to get out of the way now." Sammy paused and took a deep breath...

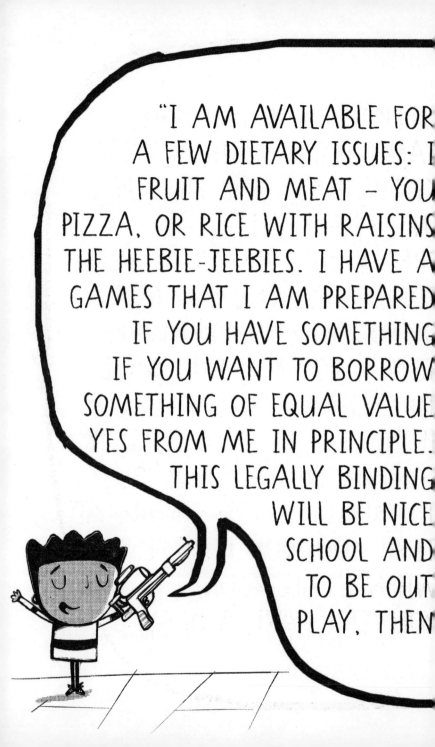

LEEPOVERS, BUT I HAVE
CAN'T EAT ANYTHING WITH
KNOW, HAM AND PINEAPPLE
N - FRANKLY IT GIVES ME
PRETTY BIG LIBRARY OF VIDEO
TO LEND TO YOU, BUT ONLY
OF EQUAL VALUE TO SWAP.
TOYS - AGAIN IF YOU HAVE
TO EXCHANGE - THEN IT'S A
IF YOU'RE PREPARED TO SIGN
CONTRACT THAT SAYS YOU
TO ME WHEN YOU SEE ME AT
THAT YOU WON'T PRETEND
WHEN I CALL ROUND TO
YOU, SIR, HAVE A DEAL."

Sammy smiled, pulled a piece of paper out from his pocket and waved it at Pete. "Now sign here!"

"Do you mind?!" a girl on a bike suddenly yelled out, just managing to avoid skidding into them both. She parked outside KostKutters, the local corner shop and secured her bike to a rack.

"Sorry, just hanging with my friend," Sammy apologized. The girl ignored him and started typing a message on her phone.

"You're exhausting, Sammy." Pete sighed. "I'm going in the shop now. Please don't follow me in – I'm a little scared." And with that he opened the door to KostKutters and headed inside.

Meanwhile, in another part of town, a very different sort of shopping trip was taking place. The Blodder Brothers' van pulled to a screeching halt outside the Bank and to the surprise of the few onlookers, five Prince Charleses burst through the doors with weapons in hand. There were gasps and screams as customers put their hands over their heads and hit the ground.

Baz marched up to the cashier and, without saying a word, handed over a bag and slapped a piece of paper down on the counter. The cashier gulped, unfolded the note and read it. He looked at the bag he'd just been given and read the note again.

"I'm afraid this is a bank, sir," he said politely. "We don't sell parsnips, onions or any of those 'fancy mint chocolates', nor do we stock copies of *Woman's Weekly*."

"WHAT?"

Baz cried, snatching the paper back and quickly reading it. "This ain't mine. It's a shopping list!"

"One suggests sir might have more luck at a supermarket." The cashier smiled.

"Those kids!" Baz said loudly. "We must 'ave got the notes mixed up when we bumped into each other."

"Baz, tell me it don't 'ave your fingerprints on it?" Blake growled beneath his mask. "If they 'ave a threatening note with *your* handwriting and *your* fingerprints we could all go to prison for a very long time."

The cashier continued to smile, calmly moved his arm under the desk and hit the alarm button.

"EVERYONE OUT!"

Baz bellowed to his brothers and started to run towards the door. "BACK TO THE HIDEOUT!"

"Well I must say, I expected better manners from Prince Charles." The cashier tutted.

4 p.m.

"What a weird boy," Pete muttered under his breath as he walked through the aisles. KostKutters was one of those amazing local shops that sold everything from cornflakes, to nuts and bolts and all that's in-between. Pete grabbed a pair of sunglasses, popped them on and stared at himself in the mirror. "I'm cool," he said eyeing up the novelty glasses in the display mirror.

The bell above the shop door rang out and Sammy casually walked in – still clutching his water pistol – as he pretended to browse for items.

Pete turned around and sighed loudly. "You just don't give up, do you?"

"Nope! So, do you want a turn with my water pistol? That's what friends do, you see?"

"No! I just want to get this done and go home."

"Or I could blast you again ... or we could fire it at that man?" Sammy said, pulling back the loading mechanism.

"Hey, you boys want something?" Kosto said, putting down his paper and peering at them. Kosto had run the shop for as long as Pete could remember and he always sat at the counter in his shirt, reading the paper and drinking tea, no matter what time of day it was.

"No! NO ONE'S GETTING BLASTED!" Pete yelled out.

"What?" Kosto asked loudly, thinking that Pete was talking to him.

"Be quiet!" Pete cried out.

"OK." Kosto gulped.

Pete – still followed by Sammy – walked up to the counter and handed the folded note and bag-for-life over to Kosto. "Would you mind helping me find some of the things on my list?" Pete said absent-mindedly.

Kosto picked up the note and read it to himself.

Give mE all youR moNey or I'll Let you have it.

Kosto looked at the two boys in front of him; one was wearing dark glasses, the other had his finger on the trigger of what looked like an enormous machine gun.

This was a robbery. He was in the middle of a stick-up. Kosto trembled with fear.

"Ignore my ... acquaintance," Pete said
with a reassuring smile.

"Don't worry – you're safe ... as long as
my finger doesn't slip!" Sammy joked in a
"core-what-am-I-like" kind of voice.

Pete turned to Sammy and said through gritted teeth, "Now listen here, sunshine: I do not need an annoying little kid hanging around with me. It's a very generous offer of friendship, but no thank you. Now if you'll excuse me, I'm going to get my parsnips and go home and watch TV."

Pete was so busy arguing with Sammy that he didn't notice Kosto emptying the till and stuffing every last drop of cash into the bag-for-life.

"OK, OK, I get the picture," Sammy sighed. He had tried his best, but it wasn't to be. He nodded quietly and, with his shoulders and head slumped, he left the shop. Finally Pete was alone again. He turned towards Kosto and went to take off his sunglasses.

"NO!" Kosto cried out. "JUST TAKE THE BAG! TAKE THE LOT IF YOU LIKE!"

"What?" Pete asked, frowning in confusion.

"WHATEVER YOU WANT – YOU CAN HAVE WHATEVER YOU WANT!" Kosto shouted, shakily handing him the bag-for-life. "What sweets do you like?"

"Fizzy cola bottles ... argh!" Pete yelped as Kosto threw five bags at him.

"Take it all!" Kosto hurled a bunch of bananas, a copy of *Caravanning Weekly*, four tins of pilchards and a family-size bag of Mini Cheddars at Pete's head before ducking behind the counter.

"What about the parsnips?" Pete shouted in confusion.

There was a few seconds of silence, then two parsnips flew over the counter and bounced along the floor.

I think Kosto may have lost the plot, Pete thought to himself as he scooped up the groceries and slowly walked out of the shop. *I don't remember bananas being on the list ... I didn't even pay for any of this. Maybe I've won a competition, like Kosto's one millionth customer or something? Still, I think he needs to lighten up with his style. It's almost like he was scared of me...*

Pete put the shopping down on the pavement and opened the bag-for-life so that he could arrange all of the groceries neatly into it.

"WHAT ON EARTH?!"

Pete shrieked and whipped off his sunglasses. The bag was stuffed full of ten, twenty and fifty pound notes. "There's got to be hundreds, maybe thousands in here..." he whispered to himself as he rummaged through the bag. Then he found a crumpled piece of white paper.

Give mE all youR moNey or I'll Let you have it.

"That's not my shopping list," Pete said in a panic. He read the note again. Then he remembered Sammy and the water pistol. Pete's blood ran cold. Had he accidentally just robbed a shop? "OH NOOOOO," he yowled. "OH-NO-OH-NO-OH-NO-OH-NO," he repeated over and over again.

He quickly turned and knocked on the door. "Mr Kosto, it's me, Pete, from down the road. I think there's been a bit of a mix-up... Coooo-ee! Anyone there?" he called out. But Mr Kosto didn't open the door, he didn't take his money back and have a right good belly laugh about it all. There was silence. It was awful, and then there wasn't silence, which was worse.

DinGALinGALinGALInG!

The sound of the burglar alarm wailed through the neighbourhood. Pete stood there for a second. "What am I going to do?" he said to himself and paced around in a circle. "The police are bound to come – wait, that's it, the police! I'll just explain what happened and they'll see it's a misunderstanding and we'll all have a chuckle about it. I just need someone to back up my story, I need a witness, I need a—"

"A friend?" Sammy said, appearing from behind the bus stop outside the shop.

"Sammy, my old chum. Funny, I was just thinking that maybe I made a mistake about you. After all, you seem like a good fellow. How would you like to help a friend out?"

"A what?"

"A friend. Oh, wait … you didn't think I was being serious with all that 'go away' stuff, did you? I was just, you know, larking around, having a laugh with my pal."

"Pathetic." Sammy shook his head. "You know what to do," Sammy said, unfurling the friendship contract and holding out a pen. "Initial here, here … and here, and sign and date here."

"Fine," Pete said, grabbing Sammy's pen and signing away.

"Excellent! Glad to have you aboard. Now what can I do for you, *friend*?"

"Yes … well, I won't lie to you, there's been a bit of a hiccup. I think I … well, I think *we* may have just robbed that shop."

"Oooh, that's *is* awkward," Sammy said, scrunching up his nose. "OK, well instead of waiting for the police to get here and arrest you and quite possibly me, why don't we just call them and let them know what's what? Then maybe we could head back to yours for squash and biscuits?"

"Good plan, good plan." Pete agreed.

"Imagine if we both went to prison!" Sammy laughed.

"Yeah … imagine." Pete laughed nervously.

"We need to borrow a phone," Sammy said and looked around. "I think that girl on the bike had one … ah, there she is!" Sammy pointed his water pistol in the girl's direction. Unfortunately, she had watched the hold-up from outside and was now desperately trying to unlock her bike to make a hasty getaway.

"AAAARGH!"

she squealed and dropped her phone and bike lock on the ground before running away and shouting, "you can have my bike too!"

"No-no-no-no! It's only a water pistol!
It's all just a big—OK, there she goes...
Here's a tin of pilchards for your troubles!"
Pete shouted, feebly rolling it along the
pavement towards her.

"I'm going to have to stop pointing this
thing at people aren't I?" Sammy said,
looking at the water pistol.

"Yeah, I think that might be a good idea." Pete held his head in his hands. "So, just to be clear, we've robbed a shop and mugged a child. I'll be honest: I've had more relaxing afternoons."

"We'll give it all back to her once this mess has been cleared up," Sammy said. "Just dial 999 – the sooner, the better."

Pete grabbed the phone and typed in the number. "Ooh, it's ringing! Yes, hello. Police please... Yes, I'd like to report a robbery."

"Two," Sammy mouthed.

"Two robberies," Pete continued. "A phone got stolen and then a bike – oh, and a shop has been robbed ... so actually that's three robberies to report... Well, spree is a very strong word." Pete winced. "Err ... yes, I did see the whole thing... Was there a gun?" He stroked his chin and looked at the pistol. "I'm going to say yes to that. I did see who did it ... it was me. I am the robber. Well there's a couple of us actually. Say hello." Pete gestured to Sammy.

"Hi!" Sammy shouted chirpily.

"Yes, I guess he is my accomplice... Mainly just cash and pilchards. These things just sort of happen, don't they? Yes, this is the stolen phone I'm speaking on... Well, all I have to say is that we're utterly responsible for nothing more than a complete misunderstanding... Hello … hello? Oh, I think the battery's gone," Pete said, swiping away at the screen.

"How much did they get?" Sammy asked.

"YOU'RE UTTERLY RESPONSIBLE?!"

the police sergeant on the other end of the phone yelled. "Hello, HELLO?! They've hung up. Get the Chief. We have a situation!"

Suddenly a door swung open and a woman came charging in. She had slick black hair, thin red lips and a pointy nose and was carrying a coffee cup the size of a vase. Her face was shiny with sweat and she looked really angry. This was Chief Jones, head of Barnet's Serious Crime Unit.

"DID SOMEONE SAY SITUATION? WHERE?"

she boomed.

"KOSTKUTTERS!" the sergeant cried.

"Wait, that's a sweet shop, isn't it?" she yelled. Chief Jones was a yeller. It had been one of the first things they taught her in police training: how to yell and how to say, "What's all this then?"

"Actually, they sell a surprising selection of goods, from parsnips to nuts and bolts," a passing policeman added.

"GOOD BACKGROUND INTEL!"

the Chief bellowed. She took a moment and paced up and down, before staring out of the window. "But who would target KostKutters…?"

The room fell silent as everyone had a bit of a think.

"Wait!" Chief Jones cried out. "I've seen this before… There's only one gang brazen enough to rob a local shop in broad daylight. The Blodder Brothers must be back in town. Well, not on my watch. This time I'm going to put them away for life!

THEY WON'T KNOW WHAT'S HIT THEM!"

5 p.m.

"Maybe if we go to the police station in person—" Pete reasoned, tapping the phone to try and make it work again—"they'll see it's a couple of kids and it'll all be fine."

"Yeah ... probably!" Sammy agreed. "I mean, we only accidentally stole a huge bag of cash, sunglasses, some food, a magazine, a mobile phone and a little girl's bike, right?"

Pete nodded and started shaking with terror. This was definitely the sort of thing that would make parents explode with anger, even the really cool ones who let you call them by their first name. Suddenly Pete wondered if going to prison might be less scary than going home and facing his parents. Pete looked at Sammy. Sammy looked at Pete.

"The sooner we go the better," Pete said and put the phone with the growing collection of items in the bag-for-life, before twisting the top of the bag around to hide the huge stash of money.

"The police station is quite a long way away. Maybe we should ... you know..." Sammy said, looking at the small pink bike that had a sparkly basket, ribbons on the handlebars and fluorescent lights on the back wheels.

"Sammy, no. I don't want to actually steal it!"

"But it would be quicker – and the faster we get to the station, the faster we can sort this whole mess out."

Pete stood in silence for a few seconds. "OK ... but how are you going to fit?"

"Fit in what?" Sammy asked.

"I really don't know why I had to sit in the basket!" Sammy complained. His knees were under his chin and the water pistol was wedged between his legs.

"YOU'RE SMALLER!"

Pete yelled. His feet whirled round and round on the pedals, but they were only achieving a brisk walking pace at best.

"Oh, I see. Is that how it's going to be? *I'm smaller.* I'm always going to lose that argument, aren't I?"

"Stop complaining and be careful where you're pointing that pistol. I really don't want any other misunderstandings," Pete said, clutching the bag-for-life in one hand, steering with the other.

"Nice day for it," an elderly gentleman called, nodding to Pete and Sammy as he overtook them on his mobility scooter.

"PEDAL FASTER!"

Sammy yelled. "This is embarrassing!"

Pete gritted his teeth and put everything he had into pedalling.

At the other end of the high street a police convoy of motorbikes, vans and cars of every shape and size, screeched to a halt. High above, a helicopter was scanning the area. Down below, Chief Jones climbed out of a car and inspected a shopfront. The door to KostKutters flew open and a very distressed Kosto burst out.

"Oh, thank you. There has been a crime, a terrible crime!"

"Mr Kosto, I'm Chief Jones – head of Barnet's Serious Crime Unit. I'm told there were two suspects. Can you describe them for me?"

"One was wearing sunglasses and a bow tie. The other one had … a gun," Kosto whimpered.

"I overheard them talking," a tiny voice interrupted from behind them. "The little one with the gun is called Sammy. Him and the other boy stole my phone and my bike and headed that way," she said pointing down the street. "I'm Penelope by the way."

"A little girl's phone and bike," Chief Jones said, shaking her head and writing the information down. "Anything else, Penelope?"

"Yes," she gulped. "The other one threw a tin of pilchards at me – well it was more of a roll than a throw, but it was pretty scary, I hate pilchards."

Everyone gasped in horror.

"Pilchards are pretty disgusting," Chief Jones said, quietly attracting all sorts of nods of agreement.

A policeman suddenly bounded over. "Ma'am, we've just received these pictures – they're from the security cameras." He showed the Chief a grainy picture of Pete and Sammy.

"I knew it. There's only one gang around here who wear bow ties…" Chief Jones narrowed her eyes. "The Blodders. I want this picture on every TV in the land.

I WANT THIS TOWN ON LOCK DOWN!

You two—" she pointed at Kosto and Penelope—"I need you with me."

"Stop the bike!" Pete cried out as he struggled to balance the huge bag of cash on his back while gripping the bike frame between his legs. It seemed only fair that Sammy had a go at pedalling too, even if he insisted on hanging on to his water pistol while steering.

"What, what is it?" Sammy asked and skidded to a stop.

Pete got off and examined the front wheel. "Just as I thought, we've got a puncture," Pete said. "I told you not to do that one-eighty turn past Greggs. You were asking for trouble."

"There was a pigeon in the road!" Sammy replied. "I didn't have much choice."

"Either way, it's not going anywhere now," Pete said and kicked the baggy tyre. "Maybe we should stash it somewhere and come back for it later? Give me a hand pushing it."

Sammy and Pete manoeuvered the bike off the road and out of sight behind some bins in an alleyway. Pete looked at Sammy, who was still holding the water pistol.

"Maybe you should leave that thing here too?"

"*Ooh,*" Sammy moaned.

"Bad things have happened because of it!"

Sammy begrudgingly agreed and hid the water pistol with the bike.

"Back in a mo," Pete said suddenly before disappearing from the alley.

"What on earth?" Sammy called out, running after him. *What could possibly be so important?* he wondered, and then, he saw Pete gazing through the window of a dry-cleaner's shop. "Oh, you are kidding me," Sammy said. There, sat on the top of a counter, was a tiny TV that was showing the snooker.

"It's OK, I haven't missed anything, Shelby still hasn't taken his shot. He's just weighing up the options – what a master tactician," Pete said as he stared wide-eyed in wonder at the screen.

"You mean, in all the time since you left the house and embarked on a life of crime, no one has actually taken a shot?" Sammy asked, barely able to believe what he was saying.

"I know. It's exciting, isn't it? So tense you can almost chew on it," Pete said opening the shop door and stepping in, mesmerized by the match.

"I might have to get a lawyer to look at our contract," Sammy muttered under his breath and followed him in.

Just then, the snooker disappeared and a giant *Breaking News* logo, followed by a stern looking newsreader, appeared on the screen.

"We interrupt this programme to warn you that two armed and dangerous criminals are on the loose. The outlaws are already being dubbed The Pilchard Kid and Little Sam, and local police are now offering a cash reward for any information leading to their arrest."

At that moment, a blurry picture of Pete and Sammy flashed across the screen.

Little Sam   The PILCHARD kid

"The criminals held up a local shop, stole cash and produce, including pilchards, then stole a bike and a phone from an innocent bystander. Just one question remains: are these two the newest members of the infamous Blodder Gang?"

"This is bad," Pete said quietly and turned to Sammy. "We need to get to the station now! Why did you let me stop to—hang on, who on earth are the Blodder Gang?"

"Oh, I've seen them on that show 'Extreme Criminals' where a bloke in a very tight black T-shirt investigates bad people. The Blodder Gang is the worst."

"Oh great." Pete was trembling now.

Just at that second, the owner came in from the back of the shop clutching bags of clothes that were neatly suspended on hangers. "Can I help you two?" he said, paying no attention to the TV.

"We need to get out of here," Pete whispered to Sammy. "If he sees us on TV he'll think we're tough guys … then who knows what might happen?!"

"Agreed," Sammy said in a hushed voice and looked around the shop. "Maybe we could use some of the clothes to disguise ourselves?"

"Can I help you?" The man behind the counter asked again, still sorting through the bags.

"Yes," Sammy said to the owner, winking at Pete. "We're here to pick up some clothes."

"Yes," Pete said, suddenly twigging. "We're here to collect some disguises—

I MEAN CLOTHES!"

"What's the number please?" the man asked.

Pete thought for a second, then took a wild stab in the dark and said, "Err... 153?"

"Yep, it's right here. And you?" he asked, looking at Sammy.

"237?" Sammy said tentatively.

"Got it," the man said. "That's twenty quid please mate – are you paying together?"

"Yes." Pete smiled. "Do you have any money?" he asked Sammy.

"No," Sammy said. "Do you?"

"I'm not sure. Hold this," Pete said, passing Sammy the bag-for-life while he checked his pockets.

"Oh wait, what about the stash?" Sammy said, looking in the bag.

"I guess we could borrow some?" Pete murmured. "Here you go," he said, smoothing out a note and handing over the money. "And have a couple of tins of pilchards for your trouble." Pete placed the tins on the counter and grabbed the clothes. He hoped that the man wouldn't turn around and see the TV.

Pete and Sammy immediately started pulling the new outfits over their clothes. The man behind the counter didn't know where to look.

"Sorry, just couldn't wait to try these on again ... so clean!" Pete said.

"So fresh!" Sammy joined in as he grabbed more clothes from the bag.

"The news once again: two vicious, ruthless criminals are on a crime spree through the streets of Barnet,"

the TV blurted out.

"Sorry, this thing is really loud – I was just watching the snooker." The owner tutted and turned around just as the screen showed a picture of Pete and Sammy on a little girl's bike, waving a water pistol about.

"Local police have strongly advised that these boys are dangerous and should not be approached."

The man held his hands in the air and turned around slowly. "Please, please don't hurt me," he begged.

"Oh great, here we go again," Sammy said as he turned to Pete.

"RUUUUUUN!"

6 p.m.

Somewhere in a seedy part of town, a van snaked its way through the back alleys to an abandoned warehouse. As soon as the van came to a stop inside, its doors creaked open and smoke spilled from the exhaust. One by one, Baz, Bob, Blake, Brody, Bill and Brad tumbled out. This was a warehouse like no other – it was the headquarters of the Blodder Gang.

"You're late," came a deep voice from a dark corner.

"Sorry, Boss," Baz said, sounding tiny and meek from behind his mask.

"Funny, I've been checking the news… There's nuffin' about a bank heist – nuffin' at all. It seems that the Blodder Gang has been holding up a corner shop though," the voice snarled.

"The fing is—" Bob started to explain.

"The thing *is* that two armed criminals are going around

PRETENDIN' TO BE US!

And what's more, Old Bill are upping the reward money for their arrest every hour." A hand shot out of the darkness, clutching

THE DAILY GRIND

SMOOTH CRIMINALS

LITTLE SAM & THE PILCHARD KID

a copy of the evening paper, with a picture of Sammy and Pete on the front page. "Still ... maybe I should get these two on board, especially as they seem to be better than you lot at carrying out a simple job. Do you know what your failure means?"

"Yeah ... no pocket money this week," Baz mumbled.

"That's right, no pocket money FOR ANY OF YOU!" the voice growled.

"But, *Muuuuum*..." the Blodder Brothers cried and took off their masks.

"But Mum nuffin'," Ma Blodder bellowed and walked out into the light; her full four-foot-three-inch figure twitching with rage.

"Call yourself Blodders? Your old dad would die of shame if 'e were alive. Gawd rest his soul. Ever since he keeled over after his part in the Great Tram Robbery – Gawd rest his soul – I've been in charge of the family firm.

All I've ever tried to do was carry on his good work – Gawd rest his soul – to try and achieve what he never could – Gawd rest his soul – make this family the baddest and the best. But look what I have to work with. I'd be better off employing the real Prince Charles," she said, glaring at them.

"We're gonna get those kids, Mum," Baz said. "We'll show them who's boss. We ain't gonna be outdone by a couple of amateurs. We'll end this today." All the brothers nodded and grimaced in agreement. "We'll make you proud – and our old dad."

"Gawd rest his soul," they all muttered.

"As disguises go, I'm not sure it's the best," Pete said, checking out his outfit of Bermuda shorts and a Dundee United Away shirt in the reflection of a window.

"Well, it's better than mine," Sammy said, adjusting his top hat and pulling his maxi dress up. "Do you think we blend in?"

"It doesn't matter if we blend in. The important thing is that we don't look like us – and we don't look like the Blodder Brothers, whoever they are," Pete said. "Right, let's just make our way to the police station and explain this rather large and massively embarrassing misunderstanding and finally go home."

A few minutes later, Pete and Sammy opened the door of the station and walked up to the front desk. They couldn't see anyone, so Sammy rang the service bell.

DING DING

A close-shaved head popped up from behind the desk.

"Ah, at last!" a stout fellow with a stern face yelled.

"Argh!" Pete yelped in shock and jumped back.

"My name's Jiggins, Desk Sergeant Jiggins. And what time do you call this?"

"Well, it's nearly—" Sammy started to reply.

"I KNOW WHAT TIME IT IS!" Jiggins yelled back. "And I certainly know who you two are. I tell you what, they get younger and younger … you look like a couple of kids! Where have you been, and why are you dressed like that?"

"It's a funny story actually... I was off browsing for parsnips—" Pete began.

"I don't care about root vegetables! This is serious! Now, I suggest you stop wasting

my time and come with me so that we can begin processing you…" Jiggins said and started off down a corridor. "Hurry up!" he barked.

Sammy and Pete slowly followed the desk sergeant, cherishing their last steps of freedom.

"I suppose it was too much to just be let off," Sammy whispered to Pete. "Technically we did rob a shop and steal a bike, a phone and some clothes … I mean, we really *did* do those things, so I guess it's only fair that we go to prison. What do you think it's like?"

"I bet it's like a never-ending lunchtime of wet play." Pete sighed. "Do you think prison uniforms are striped like in cartoons?"

"I guess we'll find out soon enough."
Sammy shrugged and hung his head.

The sergeant stopped in front of a door
and jangled his collection of keys as he
searched for the correct one. He unlocked
the door and ushered the boys inside.

"Now, go in there and get your uniforms
on. I'll be back in a couple of minutes,"
Jiggins shouted and pulled the door shut.

Sammy and Pete stepped mournfully into the cell and found their uniforms, neatly folded on a bench. Sammy started to pull it on over his clothes, while Pete put the bag-for-life down on the bench.

"I'm going to be boiling in all this," Sammy moaned as he buttoned up his jacket. "Can you put my hat in your bag?"

"Sure. Wait … your jacket…" Pete said as he stopped buttoning up his own jacket and pointed at Sammy, "it looks like police clothes."

"Well, so does yours—" Sammy began.

"I'LL JUST GET YOUR HATS!"

Jiggins bellowed from the corridor. "New recruits need to be wearing full uniform!"

"New recruits?" Pete said as quietly as he could. "Sammy! He thinks we're here to join the police!"

"Oh, great! Prison was awful … thank goodness we're getting a second chance!" Sammy grinned.

"We haven't actually been to prison yet, Sammy. All we've done is sat in a room for twenty seconds and put on an oversized jacket!" Pete said, looking at the sleeves that had flopped over his hands. Suddenly the door opened again.

"Don't worry lads. You'll grow into it," Jiggins boomed. "Here you go," he said, handing the police hats to the boys.

"I'm afraid there's been some mistake," Pete began as he took the hat and picked up the bag-for-life.

"There's no mistake. It's down here on the clipboard: two new recruits starting today. The clipboard is never wrong. Now, let's begin training. I want you to pretend you're a couple of criminals and I'll show you how to handle it."

"But we *are* a couple of criminals!" Pete wailed.

"That's *very* good." Jiggins beamed. "You'll go far in the force with that level of commitment."

"No, he's right. We've robbed a shop, stolen a bike, a phone, some clothes – and that's just so far. Who knows what we'll do next?!" Sammy said trying his best to convince the sergeant. "Please, please, we want to confess!"

"Very well. Let's take you down to the actual cells," Jiggins said shaking his head.

"Really?!" Pete looked hopeful.

"No," Sergeant Jiggins whispered. "I'm acting too."

"Please, you have to listen to me, Sergeant Jiggins: we *are* criminals," Sammy begged.

"Yes, I know! And I'm taking you to your cell, you reprobates!" Jiggins smiled and winked.

"We're not acting. We really are criminals. Everything we told you is true!" Pete pleaded.

Just at that second, Sergeant Jiggins' radio bleeped into life and a frantic voice called out:

"Attention, all units, we have a Code Twelve, repeat, Code Twelve!"

"Goodness me!" Jiggins barked. "Apparently there's a couple of criminals running amok in the town; holding up shops, stealing clothes and pinching bikes!"

"A Code Twelve means all that?" Sammy muttered under his breath.

"We're going to have to cancel training.

You're needed in town. GO, GO, GO!"

"But that's us," Pete shouted. "We're the Code—!"

"That's the spirit! Yes, you're the code of the law!" Jiggins said nudging them towards the front door. "Training is over! I need you to go out and crack the case. Do you think you can do it?" Jiggins yelled, opening the door.

"Yes, I mean why not?! We're clearly a couple of policemen and definitely not a couple of kids with a huge bag of money!" Pete screamed in frustration.

"Good lads. Oh, by the way, you should be careful carrying so much money around when there are criminals about!" Desk Sergeant Jiggins said before slamming the door on Pete and Sammy.

"WHAT IS WRONG WITH PEOPLE?!"

Pete shouted, dropping the bag-for-life on the pavement outside. "We try and do the right thing, and what happens … we end up impersonating police officers!" Pete kicked an old can of fizzy pop across the street. "Maybe we should be criminals. It can't be any harder than trying to be law-abiding citizens."

"What shall we do now?" Sammy asked and put his policeman's hat on.

"Steal the Crown Jewels…?" Pete sighed. "You know, none of this would have happened if you hadn't squirted me with that gun."

"What?"

"I'm just saying…"

"Wait, you're actually blaming me for this? I wasn't on any wanted lists until you started handing over random pieces of paper to shopkeepers, mate!" Sammy shouted.

"Mate? Don't call me mate!"

"I don't want to be your mate, mate!"

"THEN STOP CALLING ME MATE, MATE!"

"MAKE ME."

"MAYBE I WILL."

"WELL, MAYBE YOU SHOULD."

"MAYBE I AM."

"MAYBE YOU CAN'T."

"THAT'S IT!" Pete bellowed.

7 p.m.

By now, an army of investigators – as well as the actual army – were swarming the streets of Barnet in search of clues. Everyone had been called in to try and stop The Pilchard Kid and Little Sam.

Meanwhile, back at Barnet's Serious Crime Unit, Chief Jones was interviewing the latest witness.

"Thank you for joining us Mr—" Chief Jones asked, looking at the man from the dry-cleaner shop.

"Steamer, Mr Steamer," he said nervously.

"Let's get started then. I have two other witnesses outside who were robbed today. It seems that you are the last piece of the puzzle. Tell me everything," she said.

"Well I was born in 1948. My mother was a simple goat herder and my father, the King of Spain…" Mr Steamer started.

"I meant about the robbery," Chief Jones boomed. "What exactly did they take?"

"A football shirt, Bermuda shorts, a maxi dress and a top hat if I remember rightly. They tried to pay with cash but I was too scared to take it. Then … they left tins of pilchards on the counter – I don't even like pilchards! Oh the humanity of it all! I've never felt so sick to my stomach!"

"Are we talking about the robbery or the pilchards?"

"Both!" Mr Steamer wailed.

"How many tins?" Chief Jones asked.

"It was hard to say, but if I had to guess, I'd say two."

"And if you had to be exact?"

"Also two," Mr Steamer said

counting his fingers.

"And which way did they go when they left the shop—?"

Just at that moment, Chief Jones' radio crackled and buzzed.

"Bravo, Zero-zero, Foxtrot, Charlie, Bambi, Banana-banana..."

"Big Banana speaking. Go ahead."

"Oh, hello, Boss. Jiggins, uh, here. The good news is that I've found our two outlaws. The bad news is, uh, they left again … wearing police uniforms. Sorry about that – bit of a mistake," Jiggins said apologetically.

"They were at the station? And they stole police uniforms?!"

There was a moment's silence at the other end of the line, then came Jiggins' response. "Yes, uh, stolen … or, if you want to put it another way, they were, uh, given them. Either way, you're looking for a couple of badly dressed coppers. One question for you, ma'am, if I may—"

"The answer to your next question is yes, you are fired," Chief Jones replied and slammed the radio down on the desk.

"I only sent him to get a couple of parsnips and now he's top of the world's most wanted list!" Mum cried at the TV.

"This is a disaster. What are we going to have for tea now?" Dad asked.

"Never mind about tea! What about your *son* being wanted by the police? There's a million-pound reward on his head," Mum said pointing at the screen.

"Dead or alive?" Dad asked.

"That's the only question you have?!" Mum barked. "We know him better than anyone else – he likes snooker and keeping himself to himself and lining his socks up in order of size and colour. That doesn't sound like your typical criminal mastermind, does it?"

"Err … what?" Dad asked.

"You're spending the reward money in your head, aren't you?"

"No…"

Mum gave Dad a look.

"OK, maybe. Two words Diane: *hot* and *tub*."

"But our son is innocent!" Mum cried.

"I know, I know, but just in case he isn't, it wouldn't hurt to go and test a few out..."

Mum was on the verge of frisbeeing a cushion at Dad's head when the TV caught their attention.

"We interrupt this interrupted news report to report some more news,"

the news reporter interrupted.

"An angry mob has formed on the streets of Barnet, demanding justice and the immediate capture of Little Sam and the Pilchard Kid. Let's go there live now." The feed switched to a reporter, standing next to a woman who was holding a pitchfork.

"Hello, madam," he said. "Is this your first time mobbing?"

"Oh yes, I'm normally at pensioner Zumba at this time, but I thought that joining in with the rest of the town and demanding justice and action seemed like more fun."

"Thank you, angry lady," the reporter replied. "More interruptions as we get them."

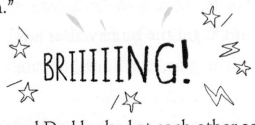

BRIIIIING!

Mum and Dad looked at each other as the doorbell rang out.

"Saved by the bell," Dad murmured to himself as Mum went to answer the door. There was a mumble and the sound of voices – more than one, maybe even more than two or three – then the living room door opened and Mum came in, surrounded by policemen.

"Look, these nice police people have come to help us. I explained that our Pete is a nice boy and that the whole thing is a misunderstanding and they said they would sort it all out."

"Phew," Dad said. "So does that mean we might get the money after all?"

"Oh for goodness' sake!" Mum shouted, throwing her arms in the air.

"All right, all right." Dad sighed. "We just want this nightmare to end, Officers…?"

"Officer Baz." Baz Blodder smiled. "And these are my … associates," he said, sweeping his hand in the direction of the rest of the Blodder Brothers.

"Don't worry—" Ma Blodder grinned as she stepped into the room—"I'm sure we can work this all out, but out of interest, where do you keep your rolling pin, or perhaps a cricket bat?"

8 p.m.

"Ow!" Pete yelled. "You hurt my hand with your hat!"

"Oh my... You tried to *hit* me." Sammy reeled with shock. "You nearly knocked my police hat off! That, sir, will never do. You must pay with your life!"

"Why are you talking like you're in a costume drama?" Pete asked.

"I don't know. I thought that was how you started a fight."

"No, I don't think so," Pete said.

"OK, shall we try name-calling instead?" Sammy asked, picking up his hat.

"I can get on board with that," Pete said. "Shall I go first?"

"All right." Sammy stood there, his fists clenched, eyes closed, ready for Pete to unleash a verbal tornado on him.

"You … you—"

"Nothing too personal by the way," Sammy interrupted.

"Oh yes. Let's leave looks, family and personality out of it," Pete agreed.

"Fair dos." Sammy nodded before reassuming his pose.

"YOU … SILLY BILLY!"

Pete said.

"Is that it?" Sammy asked.

"Well, frankly, when you take looks, family and personality out of it, it doesn't leave a lot. Do you want a go?"

"OK," Sammy said, and closed his eyes.

"YOU ... NINCOMPOOP!"

"Great," Pete said. "We all done?"

"Yep. I do feel better. Friends again?" Sammy held out his hand.

"Yep. Sorry about the whole silly billy thing," Pete said apologetically. "Oh, and the hat too."

"Not at all, I'm sorry I called you a nincompoop. Shall we go to your house?" Sammy suggested. "If we can't go to the police, let the police come to us!"

"That, my friend, is a good plan! Shall we walk?"

"It's a long way and it's getting late. Maybe we should try and get a lift?" Sammy said, looking at his watch.

"OK, here's the plan. I'll stop the next vehicle that comes down the road," Pete said firmly.

"How?" Sammy asked.

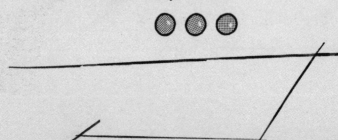

Pete stood poised in the road – his arm stretched out in front of him and his hand up, like a policeman stopping traffic. All he needed was a car to come along. It was quiet at first, then after a few minutes Pete heard a rumble in the distance.

Maybe it's a taxi or a bus, Pete thought and craned his neck, but he couldn't see anything. The noise grew louder. *Maybe it's two buses, or a fleet of lorries.* Then the ground began to shake, manhole covers popped up and down and a shadow, like a ship coming over the horizon, loomed over him.

Pete put both his hands out, beckoning it to stop, but it kept moving towards him.

Just when it seemed too late, the enormous vehicle came to a juddering halt. Pete blinked. A long, fat, gun barrel was pressing down on his nose. As the smoke cleared, a lid popped up and a young soldier's head poked out of a tank.

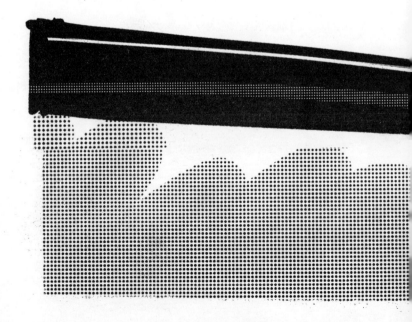

"Hello, kind sir…" Pete began and took off his jacket to reveal his football shirt and Bermuda shorts. "Don't worry. As you can see, I am not a policemen. I'm just a boy who is trying to get home."

Sammy ran up and stood next to Pete and swapped his police hat for his top hat. "Yeah, you may recognize our faces from the news—"

"Argh!" the soldier suddenly yelled, hoisting himself out of the tank and scrambling down the side as quickly as he could.

"Of course ... so now we get to add a tank to the list of items we've stolen," Pete sighed as he watched the soldier run away. "I mean, how else was this day going to end? Oh yes, that's it, with both of us actually going to prison for stealing cash, food, a magazine, a phone, a bike, clothes, police uniforms – and what was the last thing? Oh yes...

A TANK!"

Pete shouted before gasping for air.

"Relax, pal. I know how to drive a tank. We'll be home in no time." Sammy winked.

"What? Do you really?" Pete asked in disbelief. "Because you're a kid ... and most grown-ups can't drive tanks, so – and I don't want this to end in name-calling again – I'm thinking that you probably don't know how to."

"Actually, I do. Hold my top hat," Sammy said, hoisting his dress up and climbing up the tank. "I have this video game where you have to drive a tank.

It's easy, there are two levers and that's all there is to it." He peered inside the cabin then carefully lowered himself into the seat. "I told you," he yelled out, "all I have to do is—" but before he could finish, the tank jolted forward.

"Wait!" Pete yelled.

"HIT THE BRAKES!!!"

"Ah," Sammy said, popping up from the cabin. "I don't know about brakes."

"What?!" Pete cried back, chasing the tank as it slowly moved away. "Surely it's the other lever? There's only two … remember?"

Sammy ducked back down and pushed the other lever. The tank started to speed

up. "It turns out that I might need more than two levers!" Sammy shouted as he came back up. "Climb aboard! We'll figure out the brakes together."

"I can't jump onto a moving tank!" Pete said breathlessly as he tried to keep up. "It will definitely end badly!"

"End badly?" Sammy laughed.

"I THINK WE MAY BE WELL BEYOND BAD BY NOW. IN FACT, BAD WOULD BE AN IMPROVEMENT!"

Sammy leaned over the tank as far as he could and held his arm out.

"You make a good point," Pete said and took a deep breath. He whispered a prayer for his soon-to-be-double-grazed knees and jumped.

"I'm starting to think that you're not real policemen," Mum tutted. She and Dad were being tied to chairs with their backs to each other. "Real police people don't do this sort of thing."

"Yes, this is very inconvenient." Dad huffed. "Who will care for my plants if I come to a sticky end?!"

"If youse won't tell us where your son and 'is friend are, I'm afraid youse leave me no choice," Baz snarled as he tied the final knot around the chairs.

"Have we got anything we can shut these two up wiv?" Ma Blodder said, smoothing down her police uniform. "They are giving me right ear ache, and no mistake."

"I'll have a look in my bag of bad stuff,"

Brad said, opening his case and giving it a shake. It clanged and jangled like everything in there was either very heavy or very sharp – or most probably both.

Mum and Dad gulped.

"Do you know what?" Mum said breezily, "I think we'll just pipe down now. There's no need to look in that bag of yours. Me and my husband will be nice and quiet. Maybe we'll have a lovely nap."

"Oh yes," Dad said, doing a fake yawn. "All this kidnapping really takes it out of you."

"Actually it's more of a hostage situation fing than a kidnapping," Baz clarified as he took the bag from Brad.

"Oh," Mum said, looking confused. "What's the difference?"

"When we take youse wiv us to our warehouse later, that'll be a kidnapping. Until then, it's just a run-of-the-mill hostage situation," Baz replied.

Mum and Dad laughed uneasily and gulped again.

"We are not going to a drive-through!" Pete yelled from inside the cabin of the tank.

"Go on! I need some yummy, yummy nuggets! Being a notorious criminal really makes you hungry you know!" Sammy pleaded.

"NO!" Pete cried, as he jumped up and looked out of the top of the tank. "Besides which, we've got company – it seems that we've been spotted," Pete shouted, his eyes fixed on a flock of helicopters in the sky above.

The road behind them was packed with the flashing lights of police cars,

fire engines and ambulances chasing after them. Reporters with cameras were leaning out of vans, and a huge crowd of angry-looking people were also running alongside the vehicles. Some were holding signs saying, LOCK THE PILCHARD KID AWAY! or BARNET SAYS NO TO HULABALOOS! and GOLF SALE – THIS WAY! It seemed like the whole town was out in force and Pete and Sammy had somehow become the stars of a bad movie. Pete shuddered. This was going to take some explaining.

"OK, we're nearly there… We might as well keep going. You need to go straight over at this roundabout," Pete shouted down to Sammy and pointed the way.

Sammy hit the lever and yelled,

"FULL STEAM AHEAD!"

The tank suddenly charged through the middle of the roundabout, annihilating several beds of pansies, two bushes and a tree.

"When I said 'straight over', I didn't mean to actually drive over it!" Pete cried and picked the leaves out of his hair.

"Oh, oops!"

"Have you found the brake yet?" Pete asked as calmly as he could.

"I've narrowed it down to three buttons," Sammy shouted. "There's a red one, a blue one and a yellow one… What's your favourite colour?"

"I don't have one!" Pete shrieked.

"What?! Everyone has a favourite colour."

"Fine … if I had to choose, it'd be pink."

"Pink?!"

"The pink ball is worth six points in snooker—" Pete began.

"THERE ISN'T A PINK BUTTON!"

Sammy yelled.

"You didn't ask me to choose a button. You asked me what my favourite colour

141

was!" Pete hollered back. "Sammy! Make a decision, and quick!"

"OK, you're right," Sammy shouted. "Don't worry, I've got this. Eeny, meeny, miny—"

"Sammy!" Pete cried.

"What?"

"LOOK OUT!"

9 p.m.

Mum and Dad's living room began to shake and wobble as if there was an earthquake. Pictures rattled, the best china juddered in the cabinet and dust fell from the ceiling. Suddenly, there was a noise that sounded like a giant metal robot had farted and fallen over. Ma and the Blodder Brothers ran to the living room window and watched as a gigantic tank rolled to a stop in the small front garden.

Hundreds of people were closing in fast on the house, cars pulled up outside and helicopters circled in the skies above.

"What's happening, are my tulips all right?" Dad cried out in anguish.

"Never mind that, Malcolm. Now's our chance!" Mum whispered. "Let's make a break for it while they're not looking."

The Blodder Gang were indeed quite distracted by the fact that Barnet's entire police force were surrounding the house, making it impossible for them to escape.

"Ma!" Baz shrieked.

"WHAT DO WE DO?"

"Easy. We'll slip out the back door and blend in with the rest of the coppers—"

But it was too late. Pete and Sammy suddenly ran into the living room, followed by Chief Jones, a couple of police divisions, a hysterical shop-keeper, a little girl and an upset dry-cleaner.

"Mum!" Pete cried.

"Son!"

"ARREST THAT WOMAN!!"

Chief Jones bellowed.

"Eek!" Mum screamed.

"No, not that one – the short one in the top hat and dress!"

"Who are you calling short?" Sammy shouted and pointed to his top hat.

"Did you remember the parsnips?" Mum shouted.

"Not now, Mum!"

"Did you see my tulips? Are they OK?" Dad moaned as he struggled in his chair.

"Not now, Dad—hang on, why are you both tied up?"

"SILENCE!!!"

Ma Blodder yelled out and fired a gun into the ceiling. The sound echoed around the living room like a thunderbolt, making everyone's ears ring.

Ma stared at Chief Jones. Chief Jones stared at Ma. "No one move," Chief Jones said hesitantly. "She has a gun!"

"Yes, I think we got that," Sammy said.

"Oh great. First the tulips, now the ceiling," Dad sighed.

"Right, that's it! I've had enough!" Pete shouted, his face flushed. He looked Ma Blodder square in the eye and said,

"PUT THE GUN AWAY BEFORE I AM FORCED TO TAKE THINGS INTO MY OWN HANDS!"

"*What?*" Ma Blodder said. She wasn't used to being threatened by anyone, let alone a kid.

"I said … put … the … gun … away," Pete said again, slower and more deliberate this time.

"You don't scare me... you're just a kid!" She laughed and turned around to her sons who looked a little nervous.

"Just a kid?" Pete continued. "Would just a kid rob a shop, escape from the police and steal a tank? I may be just a kid, but I've done more infamous things in the past two hours than you've done in a lifetime. Look around you. I have the entire police force after me, not to mention the army and TV stations from all around the world. So ask yourself; who should be more scared here … me or you?"

The Blodder Brothers started edging towards the door.

Ma Blodder gulped. "We'll be off then, shall we? Looks like you've got this covered, Chief – we'll just head back to our squadron."

"Not so fast!" Chief Jones interrupted. "Something fishy is going on here."

"Wait!" Sammy suddenly yelled and pointed at Baz. "I recognize that man!"

"I fink youse must be mistaken," Baz Blodder snapped. "We're nuffin to do with these two kids. I just bumped into them and I must have picked up the wrong note. I have their shopping list and they—"

"Have a note threatening to rob a bank," Pete jumped in, showing Chief Jones the piece of paper, "which I bet is full of your fingerprints." Pete grinned.

"Oops," Baz whispered.

"Stop talking!" Ma snarled.

"I knew it!" Chief Jones boomed. "The only place any of you are going is to a cell. You're all under arrest!"

"If I could just explain," Pete started. "We thought we had given Kosto my shopping list and he thought we were robbing the place." Pete held up the bag-for-life. "Sorry, Kosto. Here's all of your money back. We'll pay for the tins of pilchards too."

"WHAT?!" Kosto yelled, his ears still ringing. "I can't hear a thing!"

"My water pistol didn't help either," Sammy said. "Every time I waved it around people got the wrong idea."

"You mean it wasn't real?" Penelope asked.

"No. Your bike is safe by the way – we hid it in an alleyway with my water pistol." Sammy dug around in the bag-for-life and handed Penelope the phone. "Here's your mobile too, but the battery ran out. Sorry about that."

"That's OK," Penelope said.

"We also borrowed disguises so that we could get to the police station and hand ourselves in. Here's your clothes back, Mister," Pete added, pulling off his football shirt. Sammy too took off the top hat and dress.

"Oh, thank you," Mr Steamer said.

"When we got to the police station, they told us to put uniforms on. We thought that we were putting our prison uniforms on, but somehow we ended up dressing up as policemen. So, we're sorry. We didn't mean for any of this to happen; this was just one day that got a little out of hand." Sammy shrugged.

"If you need to cuff us then go ahead," Pete said, holding out his arms and waiting to be arrested. Sammy did too. Both boys looked very sorry for themselves.

Chief Jones sighed. "Cuff them."

10 p.m.

An hour later, the boys were sitting on the sofa in Pete's living room, eating biscuits and sipping orange squash. They smiled at each other – it had been quite a day. Chief Jones had arrested the Blodder Gang and taken them to prison, and not long after that the crowds had slowly left the small house in Barnet.

"Yes, hello… I'd like to make a claim on the house insurance please," Dad barked down the phone. "Well, firstly I was held hostage, then a tank ran over my front lawn and a gangster blew a hole in my ceiling… No, this isn't a joke… Hello?"

Chief Jones suddenly appeared at the living room door.

"HELLO AGAIN, BOYS!"

Pete and Sammy jumped up from the sofa, sending their juice and biscuits flying.

"It's OK, you're not in trouble," Chief Jones boomed. "I just came back to say sorry about making you two top of the most wanted list and all that. It just goes to show that one minute you can be off to the shop and – if you're not careful – the next minute you can be a wanted criminal!"

"Haha..." Pete chuckled nervously as he and Sammy sat back down. "Well, I suppose these things just, err, happen, don't they?"

"I don't mind saying it, I'm going to miss that dress," Sammy said. "The whole dress-top-hat combo must be coming back into fashion soon though, right?"

"So, now that Kosto has got his money back and everything else has been returned," Pete continued, "does that mean we're ... off the hook?"

"Yes. Penelope's bike was where you said it would be and we've returned it to her. Oh yes, that reminds me – I thought you might want this back," she said to Sammy and handed a bag over to him.

"YES!!! MY WATER PISTOL!"

he shouted.

"Also…" Police Jones mumbled, "I wanted to thank you for helping us finally apprehend the Blodder Gang."

"You're welcome," Pete said quietly.

"Anyway…" Police Chief Jones continued in her normal booming voice, "just be careful when you go shopping again and make sure you STAY OUT OF TROUBLE!"

And with that she headed out of the door.

"Yes, ma'am." Sammy mock-saluted when she had left the room.

"PEEEEEEEEETE?"

Mum shouted from the kitchen. "Is your friend staying for tea?"

Pete had never had a friend over for tea before. "Will that be OK with your mum? You know, staying for tea at a friend's house?" he asked Sammy.

"Oh yes. Although I should probably call and ask though just to be sure … and also tell her that I'm not the hardened criminal she may have seen on TV."

"Great!" Pete smiled. "Yes, Sammy is staying for tea," he shouted back to Mum.

Mum decided to play it cool. "Open the fizz!" she shouted. "Our snooker-loving bow tie-wearing son finally has a friend! I'm so happy I could cry! Where are the party balloons?"

Muuuuum." Pete winced.

"So we're friends then?" Sammy asked.

"Of course! How on earth could I ever explain what happened today to someone else?" Pete smiled. "Plus, you can watch the snooker with me – Mark Shelby may be about to take his first shot – and I can tell you everything I know about it."

"Wow, lucky me..." Sammy sighed. "Although, frankly, after the day I've had, a bit of peace and quiet would probably do me good."

"PEEEEEEEETE?"

Mum called out again. "Do me a favour. Can you go back to KostKutters and swap this parsnip? It's a bit soft and rubbery. There's nothing worse than rubbery parsnip surprise," Mum said. "Dad will run you down there, but take Sammy with you, to keep you out of mischief."

"PLEASE TELL ME YOU ARE JOKING!"

Pete cried, flinging his arms in the air.

By now the angry mob had gone home for a cup of tea and the AA man had taken away the tank with a tow truck. If it hadn't been for two deep trenches in the garden, you'd never have known an armoured vehicle had been there. Dad drove through the quiet streets and pulled up outside Kostkutters. Pete and Sammy hopped out of the car.

"I should probably sign that contract again," Pete said sheepishly.

"Why?"

"Well, I sort of signed it using the name Mickey Mouse… Sorry." Pete shrugged.

"Haha!" Sammy chuckled. "I don't blame you. It was a bit full on I guess. In fact—" Sammy pulled out the contract and tore it up—"I don't need a piece of paper to say that you're my friend." He grinned.

Pete and Sammy opened the door to KostKutters, two best friends with a parsnip and a brand-new bag-for-life in hand.

Kosto put his newspaper down. "Oh, crikey heck, not you two again."

"Honestly, you don't need to worry, I promise."

"WHAT?"

Kosto yelled and stared at Dad sat in the car with the engine running.

"His ears must still be ringing," Sammy pointed out.

"I've come to swap this," Pete said loudly, pointing a parsnip at him. "I need to swap it, it's RUBBERY."

"WHAT?" Kosto yelled back.

"THIS IS RUBBERY!"

Pete and Sammy shouted together.

Kosto took one look at the pointy vegetable.

"THIS IS A ROBBERY?!"

he whimpered.

Then, without hesitating he emptied the entire till of cash back into the bag-for-life and hit the alarm.

READ THIS LAUGH-A-MINUTE ADVENTURE THAT IS TRULY OUT OF THIS WORLD.

Best friends Freddy and Sal have accidentally started a SPACE WAR with Alan, a grumpy alien brain muncher from Planet Twang. Soon the police, NASA and world leaders are getting involved and Freddy is about to become the MOST FAMOUS KID in town for all the wrong reasons.

"FULL OF ADVENTURE AND TERRIFICALLY GIGGLESOME." ALEX T. SMITH

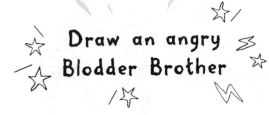
Draw an angry
Blodder Brother

1. Start with the body.

2. Add a head, two arms
   and two legs.

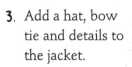

3. Add a hat, bow
   tie and details to
   the jacket.

4. Draw the eyes, a
   nose and a mouth.

5. Add as much stubble as you like. Et voilà!

Pete's top tips for a perfect disguise

◉ Find an item of clothing that adds to the sense of occasion, like a waistcoat, a long shirt or a bow tie.

◉ Sunglasses are exceptionally good for looking cool.

◉ Mix and match your clothes – a football shirt goes pretty well with Bermuda shorts.

◉ Fashion a uniform to make yourself look super official.

How to track a master criminal, by Chief Jones

- Demand intel, intel and more intel!

- Address everyone in a LOUD BOOMING VOICE.

- Ask inquisitive questions like, "What's all this then?"

- Scare the living daylights out of people by suddenly appearing in doorways.

Make a MOST WANTED poster

1. Grab a piece of paper and a pencil and write MOST WANTED at the top of the paper.

2. Think of a funny thing that you or a friend have done in the past and may be "wanted" for, and write it under MOST WANTED.

3. Draw a picture of you or your friend looking shocked.

4. Think of a funny nickname that sums up the thing you have done and add the name below the picture.

TOM McLaughlin

My name's Tom, I'm the fella who wrote and illustrated the book (illustrated is just a posh way of saying I drew the pictures). I'm here to tell you a little bit about myself. I used to be a cartoonist for a newspaper, it was my job to draw cartoons of prime ministers and Presidents. After that I started writing and illustrating my own books. I like football, fizzy sour sweets, laughing lots, sausages, staring out of the window and writing books. I have a silly children, three wives and a lovely dog ... no hang on, I mean I have a silly dog, three children and a lovely wife.

Find out more at **www.tommclaughlin.co.uk**
www.walker.co.uk